Mr. Bloom's Nursery

Meet the Veggies!

BANTAM BOOKS

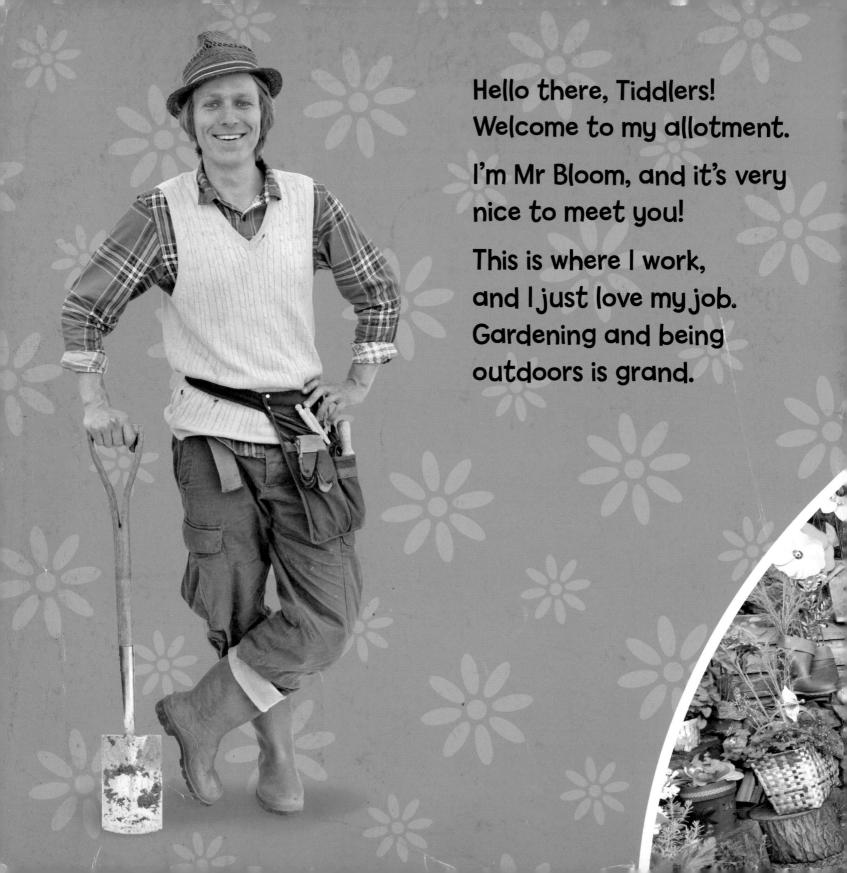

Hello there, Tiddlers!
Welcome to my allotment.

I'm Mr Bloom, and it's very
nice to meet you!

This is where I work,
and I just love my job.
Gardening and being
outdoors is grand.

I'd like to show you around and then introduce you to my Veggie friends, who are waiting inside the nursery. They can't wait to meet you!

Are you ready? Well, let's get started . . .

Let's look around the allotment first. Can you see all the plants and colourful flowers? I grow all sorts of tasty fruit and vegetables out here.

Having all these flowers around attracts a lot of insects, which is a very good thing. There are buzzing bees that carry pollen from flower to flower. Pollen helps these flowers make seeds to grow more plants!

It's so much fun when you Tiddlers come to help me. There's always such a lot to see and do!

There are plenty of seeds waiting to be sown. Then we must make sure they have enough water to drink, so that they grow into big, strong plants.

And we need to pick the fruit and vegetables as soon as they're ripe and ready. Don't these apples look delicious!

Lots of fruit and vegetables can be eaten straight away, but some you can keep for later. We've wrapped these yummy apples in newspaper, to help keep them from going bad.

Ah, and here's Compo, my amazing Compostarium. He lets me know when he's hungry, with a **twirl** of his fans and a **ring** of his bells! We can feed him with some of our leftovers and scraps.

Compo gives me all the things I need to get my jobs done. Sometimes they're a bit unusual, but they always work!

Now, shall we head inside the nursery to meet the Veggies? Come on, let's go!

This is Joan the Fennel. She's full of fantastic ideas and likes to try out new things all the time, even hairstyles!

Joan is playful and she loves to dress up and put on a performance! She's always organising a catwalk show or dancing competition for you Tiddlers to watch.

Are you ready to meet Raymond the Butternut Squash? He's brave and bold, but he can also be a little bit clumsy sometimes!

Raymond loves to laugh and have a cuddle with you Tiddlers. He's also really rather ticklish!

Here's Margaret the Cabbage. She is gentle and quiet, but she also loves to go on amazing adventures!

Margaret is very creative and has a big, colourful imagination. The pictures she paints are really good!

Next let me introduce Colin the Runner Bean, before he races away. He's always whizzing around and loves doing stunts on his scooter!

Colin has endless enthusiasm and energy. His favourite thing to do is dress up like the superhero, Captain Asparagus!

Now say hello to Sebastian the Aubergine. He's French and loves the finer things in life, like art and poetry.

Another thing Sebastian loves is singing, especially before bedtime. Whatever the occasion, he has a song to suit!

It's time to meet the Wee MacGregors, my little bunch of mischief-making Radishes. They live in a teepee, up on a shelf.

The cheeky Wee MacGregors love to play tricks and can be a real handful, but they always work as a team and are very helpful, too.

That's not all though, Tiddlers, there's so much more to see. Don't forget the onions, potatoes and peas. They also live here, in my nursery!

We've had a busy day, how the time flies! Goodbye for now, we'll see you again very soon!

MR BLOOM'S NURSERY: MEET THE VEGGIES!
A BANTAM BOOK 978 0 857 51246 8

Published in Great Britain by Bantam,
an imprint of Random House Children's Publishers UK
A Random House Group Company.

This edition published 2013

1 3 5 7 9 10 8 6 4 2

Bantam Books are published by Random House Children's Publishers UK,
61–63 Uxbridge Road, London W5 5SA

www.**randomhousechildrens**.co.uk

Addresses for companies within The Random House Group Limited can be found at:
www.randomhouse.co.uk/offices.htm

THE RANDOM HOUSE GROUP Limited Reg. No. 954009

A CIP catalogue record for this book is available from the British Library

Printed in China

The Random House Group Limited supports The Forest Stewardship Council (FSC®),
the leading international forest certification organization. Our books carrying the FSC label are
printed on FSC®-certified paper. FSC is the only forest certification scheme endorsed by the leading
environmental organizations, including Greenpeace. Our paper procurement policy can be found at
www.randomhouse.co.uk/environment

FSC
www.fsc.org

MIX
Paper from
responsible sources
FSC® C020056